HOW OBELIX FELL
INTO THE MAGIC POTION
WHEN HE WAS A LITTLE BOY

1966 – The authors toast the future of Asterix.
(Photo PARIS MATCH / Picherie)

TO THE READER

The book you are about to read was written by René Goscinny for issue number 291 of the weekly magazine Pilote, and appeared on 20 May 1965. The magazine was part of what is often considered the Golden Age of the French comic strip, publishing the Asterix stories as serials before they appeared in album form, as well as many other strip cartoons.

That week in May 1965, the Gallo-Roman period was taken as the theme for the magazine, and the cover picture by J.L. Devaux showed the Battle of Alesia, when Julius Caesar defeated the Gaulish tribes in 52 BC. Next to the title of the magazine, the cover had a picture of Obelix carrying a notice giving the date and the number of the issue, and gloomily uttering the words, "It wouldn't have turned out like that if I'd been there!" We can be sure that it would not!

That week Goscinny also decided to open the magazine with a story telling readers just how it was that Obelix came to fall into the magic potion when he was a little boy, so that it gave him permanent superhuman strength. I drew three modest pictures to illustrate the text.

The Asterix strip cartoons had been appearing for six years at this time, and Asterix and Obelix themselves are about six years old in this story, which is told by Asterix himself. It was published in book form later, and it was with emotion, a certain amount of nostalgia, and great pleasure that I set to work again on a text by my old friend René Goscinny, creating new and more elaborate pictures.★

I only hope that readers will get as much pleasure from reading this story as I myself did from illustrating it.

★ How Obelix Fell into the Magic Potion . . . *was first published in 1989. This edition has a new cover, but is otherwise identical.*

Original title: *Comment Obélix est tombé dans la marmite du druide quand il était petit*
First published in Great Britain in 1989 by Hodder Children's Books
A division of Hodder Headline
This paperback edition first published in 2010 by
Orion Children's Books
a division of the Orion Publishing Group Ltd
Orion House
5 Upper St Martin's Lane
London WC2H 9EA
An Hachette UK company

13 5 7 9 10 8 6 4 2

Original edition copyright © Les Éditions Albert René/Goscinny-Uderzo, 1989
English translation copyright © Les Éditions Albert René/Goscinny-Uderzo, 1989
Exclusive licensee: Orion Publishing Group
Translators: Anthea Bell and Derek Hockridge

The Orion Publishing Group's policy is to use papers that are natural, renewable and recyclable products and made from wood grown in sustainable forests.
The logging and manufacturing processes are expected to conform to the environmental regulations of the country of origin.

A catalogue record for this book is available from the British Library

ISBN 978 1 4440 0094 8

Printed in Italy

GOSCINNY AND UDERZO
PRESENT

HOW OBELIX FELL
INTO THE MAGIC POTION
WHEN HE WAS A LITTLE BOY

Text by RENE GOSCINNY

Drawings and captions by ALBERT UDERZO

Translation by ANTHEA BELL *and* DEREK HOCKRIDGE

"One of these days, my boy, you'll grow up to be a big, strong warrior just like your dad!"

I was born in that little village in Armorica I've told you about so often. It was there I took my first steps, and there that I grew up. Not that I grew up much, I'm afraid. I've always been rather short, just like my father and mother.

My mother was very pretty, but so small that my father used to say, laughing a lot, she was my mini-mum. My mother pretended to be cross, and said if he wasn't careful, he'd only get a minimum dinner, but she would end up laughing too, and she always cooked us her speciality. There wasn't anything mini about that, I can tell you. It was roast boar.

We were very happy, and so were all our neighbours.

I had lots of little friends. There was Cacofonix, who wanted to be a bard when he grew up. Unfortunately, he achieved his ambition. There was Fulliautomatix, whose father made our weapons, and no end of others. I've told you about them before. But my very best friend was my little neighbour Obelix. He lived within a stone's throw of me, which wasn't always funny, since his father was a menhir maker.

Obelix was a big boy for his age – very fond of his food, very nice and very sensitive. And it may surprise you to hear that Obelix didn't like fighting. He was a bit soft. So the rest of our friends often mocked him and made him an Amita Sara*, as the Romans used to say. All Obelix did was smile in a friendly sort of way, and I sometimes had to defend him against the others.

I think that was the start of our great friendship – and during playtime Obelix always shared his favourite elevenses with me: roast boar.

* Aunt Sally

"Yoohoo! Obelix is a sissy, Obelix is a sissy!!!"

"You tease my friend and you'll have me to deal with!"

"Oh yeah?"

$$I + I = II$$
$$II + II = IV$$
$$III + III = VI$$

"Well, Obelix, who is the Roman geezer?"

"............"

I mentioned playtime just now, and I meant playtime at school, because we had lessons to do. Yes, there were schools even in BC, and our teacher was Getafix the druid. The druids who taught us had to get teaching diplomas first, and Getafix was the most diplomatic of them all. He needed to be!

The rest of us have changed a lot, but Getafix looked just the same as now, with his long, white beard and his fine, drooping moustache.

He knew all sorts of things, and I've never forgotten his lessons. He taught us geometry, and how to find the volume of a menhir. He taught us arithmetic. (If one Gaul thumps three Romans, how many Romans get thumped by six Gauls?) He taught us geography (all roads lead to Rome), and current affairs (about the heroic Gauls and Julius Caesar the Roman geezer) and natural sciences (the wild boar, its habitat and cookery), and of course he taught us Gaulish grammar.

You may think this sounds a bit boastful, but I have to admit I was quite bright at school. Well, actually I was top of the class.

But I'm afraid the same can't be said for Obelix.

Obelix was a scatterbrained, absentminded daydreamer, and he was often in trouble with the druid. So after school I went round to his place almost every day to help him with his homework. I remember his mother always gave us a lovely tea. Guess what her speciality was. Roast boar!

"Is two plus two less or more or the same as three plus one?"

"Well, it dependth if it'th boarth or punishment, Athtewixth!"

"Huh! They're always telling us
to be seen and not heard!"

ometimes the Romans attacked our village. Then we had a lovely time. There was no school, because the druid was busy brewing magic potions for our dads, who set happily off for the fight, following our young chief Vitalstatistix.

We wished we weren't little, because we'd have liked to follow in our dads' footsteps. Meanwhile, our dads were following the Romans' footsteps. Of course it's not very nice picking a fight all the time, but the Romans started it, and let's face it, Gauls do like a bit of fun and a good old punch-up.

It was a noisy scene as our dads used to her together shouting, "By Toutatis!" and "By Belenos!" and "These Romans are crazy!"

There was lots more fun when the warriors came home bearing trophies, usually Roman helmets. They slapped each other's backs and fell about laughing when they thought of the look on their enemies' faces as the Romans saw them coming.

And then, to celebrate victory, our chief organized a great banquet, with any amount of our favourite, traditional food: roast boar!

We really liked those Romans!

"Tithn't fair! It'th alwayth the gwown-upth that get to eat and have fun firtht!"

Uderzo .88

ow, one day when the Romans had attacked (our dads and big brothers had gone off, and our mums were busy roasting boars for the victory banquet), us little Gauls were in the school playground without anyone supervising us, and we were wondering what to play.

"Let's have a battle with the Romans!" said Bionix.

Bionix was the strongest boy in class. He was really tough, and he thought of nothing but handing out bumps and bruises. Everybody agreed with him except me. I asked him where he thought he was going to find Romans.

"Obelix can be the Roman!" said Bionix. "We'll be the Gauls, and Obelix can be a large body of troops."

I didn't want to play, but all the others shouted, "By Toutatis!" and "By Belenos!" and they jumped on poor Obelix, who was looking at them in great surprise. Of course I defended him, and to be honest, it was a really good punch-up.

But when the others had had enough, poor old Obelix was left sitting on the ground with a black eye and a nosebleed, sniffling.

"This can't go on," I told Obelix. "You've got to learn to defend yourself."

"Okay," said Obelix. "How?"

I thought about it, and then I had an idea. I knew the druid had gone off with the others to join in the battle with the Romans. And I knew that there was magic potion in his hut.

"We're going to Getafix the druid's hut," I told Obelix. "And you're going to drink some magic potion. Just enough for you to be able to teach the others a lesson."

"Go to the druid's hut?" gasped Obelix. "But that's not allowed! I'm scared!"

I'm afraid I have to confess that Obelix was a coward too.

ot only was he afraid of the sky falling on his head, same as the rest of us, he was scared of the tiniest little dangers too, like Romans. Still, I managed to persuade him, and although he was trembling like a leaf Obelix agreed to come with me.

To be honest, I wasn't too happy myself. I felt a bit like a boar on the eve of a Gaulish victory.

Still, the village was almost empty, and we were able to reach the druid's hut unseen.

"Hurry up, Obelix!"

"I am hurrying up! It'th my legth that won't huwwy!"

**W**e hesitated on the threshold for a moment – and then we went in. (I had to drag Obelix inside. He said he didn't really want to teach the others a lesson; after all, he said, they had a right to a bit of fun.)

It was dim inside the hut, and very impressive. The place was full of golden sickles, mistletoe, herbs, cauldrons and strange instruments.

"Let's get out of here, quick!" said poor Obelix, trembling like a boar jelly. (You make boar jelly like fruit jelly, only using wild boar instead of fruit juice.)

But there was a great big cauldron right in the middle of the hut, full to the brim with magic potion. A really enormous cauldron with a strange fragrance rising from it.

"Ssh! Don't make that noise!"

"Tithn't me making a noithe,
it'th my kneeth!"

"The magic potion! It's in that cauldron!" I whispered.

To my great surprise, Obelix had stopped objecting. He'd even stopped trembling. He licked his lips. "That smells good, by Toutatis!" he said. "I think I'll take a little drop!"

Now he'd stopped raising objections, I helped him haul himself up to the rim of the cauldron, and I told him to take a good gulp while I kept watch at the door.

And as I looked out of the hut, who did I see coming?

"Ooh, quick, tell us the rest, Uncle Asterix!"

"We had a wonderful time in those days, right, Athtewixth?"

Yes, you've guessed it: Getafix the druid! The battle was over sooner than expected. (I heard later that the Romans hadn't come to fight, they'd come to offer a truce. By the time they finally managed to explain, they'd lost the battle.)

"Obelix!" I whispered, turning back to the hunt "Hide, quick! Here comes the druid!"

I heard a "Splosh!" inside the hut, but I didn't have time to go and see what it was, because the druid marched straight past me and into his hut, smiling kindly at me. I was terribly worried about Obelix.

"Our family tradition of collecting Roman helmets is passed down from father to son!"

And then, a few moments later, I heard a cry of surprise, and I saw the druid running out of his hut with my friend Obelix in his arms. My sopping wet and very unhappy friend Obelix . . .

"This is amazing!" said the druid. "I left a cauldron full of potion and I came back to find a boy in an empty cauldron, full of potion."

Obelix, who was rubbing his tummy in a satisfied way, wasted no time. He hurried off to find out friends and tell them he'd like a return match.

*"My poor little baby! He's so fragile
and delicate already!"*

From that day on, no one ever made fun of my friend Obelix again. And that's the end of my story.

So now I must be off, because I said I'd go and see Obelix. He invited me to dinner.

I expect it'll be our favourite dish: roast boar!

ASTERIX

"It's a fat lot of good fighting you, eh, Obelix?"

"Who are you calling fat?"

The End

... or the beginning